THE ADVENTURES OF SIGI
A Day At The Beach

Written
and Illustrated

by

Candace Carson

To my sister, Tarey Ray, who always got sunburned at the beach,
To children everywhere because each and every one is special
And to Sigi, a good dog who makes my life better.

ISBN 978-0-9829864-6-2

Library of Congress Control Number: 2010916956

THE ADVENTURES OF SIGI
A Day At The Beach

Book Three

Written and
Illustrated
by
Candace Carson

Sigi and LuLu Productions

Table of Contents

Find the four-leafed clover hidden in the book,
a tiny frog, a ladybug and a buzzing bumble bee.
There's a humming bird if you take a close look
and somewhere inside, a little fly you will certainly see !

The Adventures of Sigi
A Day at the Beach

Words and COLOR

It's easy to see
who's speaking to me.

Corey is such a delight,
her words are in white.

Mr. Crab's words are in tangerine.
A pinch with his claw can make you scream !

The Pelican speaks in brown.
That's the color of his down.

The Heron's words are the color of his plume.
Grey like the whale and the fish he can consume.

The one who takes good care of me
speaks in words as green as a pea.

And I am always in yellow,
just like the sun.
Because I'm a fine fellow
. . .and lots of fun !

1

Good Morning, Corey.
I'm going to the shore.
I'll play by the sea
and hear the waves roar!

You will have lots of fun,
but I am concerned.
Wear lotion in the sun
and don't get sun-burned.

I like riding in the car.
It won't be long,
we'll be there soon.

I'm glad it's not too far
I'll have a pleasant
afternoon.

4

5

I'm off to the ocean!

But Sigi,
you need lotion!

Ouch, Ouch, Ouch! The sand is hot.
My paws really burn.
Was there something I forgot?
Too late now to return.

aahh

The water feels grand
on my burning paws.

I think here I'll stand
and take a little pause.

Wow, look at all those seashells.
They're red, yellow, blue and brown.
The wind has a "fishy" smell
that's in the air all around.

9

Hey, look at those footprints.
I wonder where they go.
I'll follow where they went,
Just for awhile or so.

Quickly look back,
can you see
Whose tracks are
following me ?

I must always be aware
and I must never forget
about the waves over there,
'Cause I don't like to get wet.

Look, those prints certainly are weird.
They move along toward that hole
Into which something has disappeared.
I'll check it out and look below.

I don't see anything from here.
I might feel something with my paw.
Yes, yes, I do feel something near.

Oh, it's grabbed me,
I must withdraw !

Pinch !

Pinch !

Ooooow !

OUCH, STOP ! Please let go !
You're hurting my toe !

18

I didn't know it was you inside.
What's wrong with you Mr. Crab ?
There's no reason for you to hide
And my paw, you should not grab !

There's something you should know.
Enter my space uninvited
and my claw and your toe
will be painfully united !

I thought you wanted to eat me.
I still think you are very rude.
How was I to know you were friendly?
You have no manners, I conclude.

Scram, little doggie, scram!
You better not delay.
Scram, little doggie, scram!
Go away, go away!

I think we can all agree
that Mr. Crab is
"crabby"! Ha Ha

21

Stop looking at my shadow !
Pay attention to where you tread !
Danger awaits, look down low.
Open you eyes and use your head !

Oh!
What is it. Is it alive?
It's so white and
round like a dish.

Its sting hurts and
will make you cry.
People call it a
Jellyfish.

I must leave and
rejoin my flock.

Do try to be
careful where
you walk.

24

Goodbye Mr. Pelican.
I'll try to be more alert.
I'll watch where I step
and then for sure,
I will not get hurt.

Watch the wave,
   you'd better dash
'cause you don't want
   to get splashed !

Won't you help me,
if you care,

Please do not let
me forget

About the waves
over there,

'Cause I don't like
to get wet!

28

Hey, look at the alligator !
Oh my, isn't that clever.
It has a tail, teeth and lots more.
Will it be here forever ?

Use suntan lotion
when it's hot

Because your nose
will start to burn.

I knew there was
something I forgot.

Now it's time
for me to return.

If I were you, I'd worry.
Your nose is already red.
I think that you should
hurry.
Your burn is starting to
spread.

My skin is
beginning to feel
the heat.

I must go
or I'll be
red as a beet!

31

What color was my umbrella?
I remember it, do you?

Was it red or green or yellow
or could it have been
dark blue?

33

Why, there you are my fine little fella!
Oh, your nose is sunburned, I'm afraid.
You must rest under the umbrella.
Keep out of the sun, stay in the shade.

A day at the beach is a fun thing to do.
You see lots of things and make some friends, too.

Always remember to wear suntan lotion
On every part of you that is in the sun.
And keep an eye on the waves in the ocean,
Unless, of course, you are prepared to run !

I'm glad we spent a day by the sea.
The hot sand on my paws made me wail
And that mean ol' crab grabbed and pinched me.
I got sunburned on my nose and tail. . .but,

Pelican told me of the Jellyfish's sting
And the Heron told me to put on lotion.

I saw shells, an alligator
    and other things.
I did not get splashed
    by waves in the ocean !

All in all it was a
    grand day, I suppose.
Except for the sand
    in my hair and my toes.

Will they remove the sand
    with a brush and comb ?

They will be tired--
    do you think they will forget ?

Do you think they will wash me
    when we get home ?

I hope not, 'cause

I DO NOT LIKE TO GET WET !

Sigi's Friends

Corey, The Monarch Butterfly

Crabby the Crab

The Brown Pelican

The Blue Heron

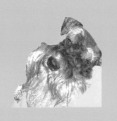

The Ones Who Care for me
...and love me, too.

Did you find the four-leafed clover in the book,
the tiny frog, the ladybug and the buzzing bumble bee?
The humming bird was inside, too--did you look?
I added a small ant and the fly was somewhere by the sea.

Books by Candace Carson

THE ADVENTURES OF SIGI Series

Moving Day
Some Days Are Better Than Others
A Day At The Beach
A Day As A Portuguese Water Dog
A Day In The Mangroves (forthcoming)

WEE LULU Series

A Good Example
Come See My House (forthcoming)

SIGI TRAVEL Series
coming in 2011

A Day in New York City
A Day in New Orleans
A Day in San Francisco